Dust in the Wind

"All are of the dust"—Ecclesiastes, 3:20

"Labor for the wind"—Ecclesiastes, 4:16

By

Donald J. Richardson

For all my teachers and all my students

Illustrations

Frontispiece: Farmer Arthur Coble and his two sons run for cover as a dust storm approaches. Cimarron County, Oklahoma—April 1936 (Arthur Rothstein/Farm Security Administration)

Dust in the Wind

Pa helped me make my first slingshot the summer I was seven. We used strips of rubber from an inner tube for the shooting part, the palm of an old leather glove for the pouch to hold the rock, and a y-fork from the branch of an elm for the part to hold in my left hand. I practiced all that summer with my slingshot until finally I got so I could knock a tin can off a corral fence post from about thirty feet away.

Then I discovered another use for the slingshot. I was walking home from school one afternoon in the fall when a cottontail jumped up out of a tumbleweed caught in the fence row beside the road. He stopped ahead of me and froze the way rabbits do, looking back at me sideways without really looking right at me.

Carefully I eased my slingshot out of my back pocket, loaded a good rock, and took aim. When he jumped up, I thought I had missed even though I'd seen the rock hit him, but then he fell over. I guess he was pretty surprised, but I was, too, that first time. I hadn't thought about my slingshot being good for much besides shooting tin cans off the corral fence posts or chasing chickens. As I hurried home with my bounty, I realized that now I could help provide food for our table, and I didn't need a rifle to do it either.

Pa and Ma had taken the farm on shares during the late twenties when I was still a baby. There had been several good years with heavy wheat harvests and the promise of more to come. All around us, when I was a boy, I would see miles of green wheat rippling in the spring breezes and later on golden stalks with the grain heavy at the top, just waiting for the threshing machines to come through and transform the wheat into money in the pockets of the sharecroppers and the owners.

Pa had sold the team of mules and bought a tractor and a bigger plow on payments in town, and Ma had insisted on things for the house, too, so it didn't look like a sharecropper's house but like a farmhouse instead. We got so we began to act and feel like real farmers even.

For miles around, farmers were buying tractors and giant three- or four-bottom plows to break the sod and plant more wheat. Gradually the view of native grasses and wild plants gave way to one of upended roots and later smoothly-worked ground. Later on the wheat fields stretched as far as the eye could see in every direction. There was money to be made; all people had to do was plant wheat, so it was little wonder that farmers and sharecroppers planted from border to border, not thinking that might be bad for the land.

Then the good years ended. There was no warning, they just stopped. The first sign was that there was no rain.

Elkhart, Kansas homestead abandoned in 1935

(National Archives)

When I was a boy, I used to get irritated at all the talk about weather. Everywhere we went, whether it was to a box supper at school or the pool hall in town, everybody talked about how hot or cold it had been, how much it had rained if it had, or whether it would if it hadn't, and how long the current spell would last before it broke, good or bad.

I've heard sharecroppers and even true farmers greet each other the same way hundreds of times. "How's the weather been over at your place?"

"Oh, pretty dry. Pretty dry. We had a little sprinkle t' other night, hardly enough to wet the rain gauge. I'd guess about five hundredths. How 'bout you?"

"'Bout the same. Sure wish this dry spell would break."

I've seen my father go out to the rain gauge of a morning hoping there had been rain during the night, even when he knew for a certainty there hadn't been, just to check it to make sure it was still there, maybe hold it up and shake it to make sure it was still working, as if it was at fault somehow.

And before you know it, when you live among people like that, you find yourself doing the same as they do without even realizing it. I got so I'd study the dust in the road every morning when I'd bring the cows in from the pasture just to see if it had sprinkled during the night and I hadn't been aware of it. And the times I noticed signs of rain that my father didn't, I was right proud of myself.

But that's how it is with people who depend on the land and their crops for a living. They get so wound up in nature that pretty soon it's nearly impossible to tell where the people stop being people and start being nature. They get so they can predict rainstorms based on the way their bodies feel, or anyway they <u>say</u> they can. I guess you've heard of people saying, "Ayup, it's gonna rain, all right; my rheumatism's acting up." Or, "My corns have been bothering me something fierce; I just know we're gonna have a gullywasher."

Most of the time I guess they're just hoping, but then there's always a time or two that they turn out to be right, and after that can't nobody talk them out of believing in their rheumatism, or corns, or whatever it is that gives them the high sign.

Mechanized farming, spring, 1935

(Kansas State Historical Society)

So it stopped raining, and everything just naturally dried up; this was in the early thirties. Later on folks called those years the dirty thirties, and they were. The dust would roll up in

clouds and come out of the distance looking like a tornado, but

when a person saw how big it was he knew this was no tornado.

A dust cloud rolls in above the town of Arlington, Kansas in

1935 (Hutchinson News)

It was worse than a tornado or even a blizzard because the

tornado is soon gone, even though it does real damage and can

kill people or livestock. It does its worst and goes on. And the

blizzard always ends, too, sometimes not for a few days, but when it's finished it leaves snow, and every wheat farmer alive will tell you how important snow is for winter wheat. But these dust storms were the worst part of nature I ever lived through.

I've read of people going through typhoons on the ocean or real heavy sea storms; I figure at a time like that a man gets as close to the bad side of nature as he possibly can what with all the wind and water and the real danger that can't be escaped. I've never been on a ship that went through a storm at sea, but I've stood on our front porch and watched that dust cloud coming, knowing there wasn't a thing I or anybody else could do about it.

It's a frightening feeling being in the face of some force like that; it reminds a person that he's only a mite in the universe, and that's not comforting. One time, after the dust had enveloped everything in its black cloud, I kneeled down and prayed right there, hoping God would be sure to see me. I guess He did as it eventually went on.

At first the dust storms were merely curiosities. Always before it had rained, and this time it would, too. People knew they simply had to believe. But faith is bought with hard currency, and as the years stretched out ahead with no relief in sight, people began leaving. The first to go were the ones who had come into the county last. They had the least to lose as they had invested the least, so when they packed up everything onto their old Model T's or Model A's, those who stayed behind were a little smug about being stronger and hardier. They knew it would take more than a couple of hard years to dislodge their roots from this Kansas soil, dry though it was.

Later on, however, the dust storms got bone-hard serious. As the years went by and prospects of a bumper crop decreased, hope became pretty forlorn in Western Kansas, something like an unmarried old-maid cousin from Cedar Rapids visiting in her new mail order clothes. The dust was in everything we did, ate, or slept in.

A deserted farmstead (Oklahoma Historical Society)

Anything left sitting for very long, even a person, soon gathered a layer of dust. If you go into a department store these days when there aren't many customers, you might see one of the clerks dusting the merchandise. When I was a boy, the women swept the dust; there was no dusting except that which came from nature. Every morning it was the same; sweep out the new layer that had sifted down in the night.

In order to get a clean drink of water from the water bucket, we had to skim off the layer of dust on top, and that was despite the damp cloth Ma draped over the top of the pail. There was no keeping clean either. Since I've left the farm and Kansas, I've grown used to a shower or a bath <u>every</u> <u>day</u>. Such a thing was simply impossible in those days. No man, not even a senator or congressman, let alone a farmer, could have afforded such a luxury back then.

And the longer one stays dirty, the harder it is to look for the best or to hope for tomorrow. Every year our faith was hammered out a bit flatter and thinner. Every year there were fewer people who had been on the land as long as Ma and Pa with nobody new coming to take the deserters' places. It looked like wheat farming was a losing business.

Rain became not only a necessity but the faith that supported our lives. If you couldn't believe that it would eventually rain, what was left? Maybe suicide. The rumor at school just before the Yankovic kids left was that their mother had gone crazy and tried to kill herself. Maybe she had. Maybe those fine particles of dirt covering the dinner table once again finally wore down her faith to the core where there wasn't anything left but desperation. Too much dust is like sandpaper; it just eats away at whatever it rubs against until finally there's nothing left.

Some people walking on the streets wore paper face masks that covered the mouth and nose; they looked like creatures from somewhere else, not like people we knew. One of the results of challenging Nature is an alienation of everything dependable. I've seen pictures of men and women in body suits meant to protect them from radiation, and they no longer bore any resemblance to people. The astronauts of the 60's wore space suits that hid their identity while making them grotesque. Even gas masks make people look as though they have just come from some interstellar craft. The strangeness is threatening and daunting.

Volunteers wearing gas masks, Liberal, Kansas

(Kansas State Historical Society)

Maybe it was hardest on the women. They stayed in those unpainted shacks that sat right level with the ground and fought nature as best they could, but they weren't equipped for such a mighty struggle. They were plain, home-grown girls from the Midwest who had jumped too quickly into becoming women, suddenly finding themselves with a husband and children that took all of their time, sucking their innards empty.

The houses—as people graciously and euphemistically called them—were not insulated, and there were sometimes visible cracks between the boards that separated the stolid, controlled lives inside from the rampant, raging life outside.

I used to lie in my bed in the night, up under the roof close to the eave and listen to the wind singing. I liked the way it changed pitch, sometimes almost playing a tune. But what if you had to stay in that house all day and all night, almost every day as the women had to do, listening to that? It's no wonder that the pictures in my mind show the women looking strained and tight, trying to smile and not succeeding, staring out from back then to today, hoping somehow to transcend their dismal state, yet knowing it's simply impossible. Everybody went crazy a little bit during those times, so I guess it's no wonder if the Yankovics' mother went crazy, too.

It was worst for the women with babies, of course. The women worked hard to take care of the babies first of all. I have watched women all my life, and there are very few—no matter how coarse—who aren't touched by babies, even other people's. I wondered at this as I was growing up. How could Ma always give me and Rachel and Billy the best pieces of fried meat or the first pieces of fresh bread or the first of anything? Didn't she want anything for herself? She did, but for her children she wanted it even more. Maybe a small part of herself had already given up on herself, but in her children lay the future, the hopes of tomorrow that she couldn't realize except through us. I wonder if she would be satisfied with what we've become? Billy was about a year old when the dust storms started, so it wasn't as hard caring for him as it would have been had he been born in 1936 instead of 1929. Rachel was born in 1927, and I was oldest, born in 1924.

It was hard for the men and the children, too, only in a different way. We children had school which for me was a daily deliverance out of ignorance into the hands of a true missionary.

How long does it take us to see such things? I used to agree with all the other kids when they said that they'd sure be glad when school ended, but secretly I never was. Now I understand just how important school was to all of us, not just for learning and education. School was a place filled with excitement, an oasis of information in a desert of ignorance. There were other kids to know, new books to read, different places to study about, and the best teacher I think school kids ever had. She was a few years younger than Ma and Pa, but beyond that there was little comparison.

Ma and Pa were our parents, and we depended on them. I loved Ma, and I respected Pa, but Miss Lehrer was an unopened, as yet unread book of attraction for me in my grade school years. There had been other teachers before her, and there were others after her, too, but she reached above everyone else in my eyes. Maybe her methods weren't up-to-date, I don't know, but I do know that she earned her $45 a month, and we all made places for her in our hearts, even the ones who really disliked school. She wasn't beautiful, I see now, and she was actually quite small. But the way she could interest us in coffee plantations in Brazil or learning about the Sumerians, which with anybody else would have been boring, was wonderful.

She was a person full of wonder: as yet unmarried, she was everything sophisticated and attractive to me, smiling and pleasant, as beautiful-seeming in character as you'd like your own mother to be, but without the need for worry that causes a child's concern. When she played the piano and sang, I was like one hypnotized. Such a woman's company some day perhaps I might be worthy of. This education was a religious experience to me, and Miss Lehrer was my high priestess.

Compared to our mothers, we had it easy. It was hard for the men, too, but not as hard as for their wives. Men lived and worked in the soil, so I'd guess they were more accustomed to dirt naturally. There weren't many clear days back then when the technicolor of the landscape returned, but when it did it was natural that the men be outside working while the women had to take a hurried glance through a smudged kitchen window pane before going on to other work inside.

Pool hall, Sublette, Kansas (Rusinow, National Archives)

The men had their pool hall in town, too, where they could

go to sit and play checkers or smoke or talk.

Pa liked to go to play pitch or dominoes and to catch up on what had been happening or just talk about the weather. He was good at pitch, and most times he'd come home with loose change he had won. He'd let me go along, too, as long as I sat quietly, not interrupting.

The women didn't have anything like that. The closest it came was the social get-togethers Miss Lehrer organized at the school where the women would sit off by themselves and talk a bit. We knew that we weren't to bother them then. Sometimes they might get together at church, too, but Roman Catholics in those days were more strict about not mixing religion and pleasure than they are today, so church-going was mostly a time for prayer and meditation, as if there were a shortage of time to meditate at home.

I didn't know all of this back then—I was only a boy—but I remember the way things were and the way people looked, and today I can re-play those images in my mind something like a stereoscope, only better because I was actually there. The memories are hard-edged like the personalities of those Kansas dirt-farmers of the thirties. And the scenes are always in drab-looking black and white or more likely, a universal gray—the gray of the dust in the air blocking out details and shading the edges of everything into everything else, like an old-fashioned tintype photograph.

I was twelve that April when I finally got the rifle I had been asking for. I had wanted it for Christmas or my birthday for several years, but Ma and Pa had always said to wait, that I wasn't old enough. The Christmas presents the year before had all looked wrong; none was a rifle, I could tell. I was disappointed, but in our family one wasn't allowed to show that much selfishness, so I pretended that everything Ma and Pa and Rachel and Billy gave me was just perfect. But in my heart I knew I'd have to go on using my slingshot for killing rabbits and other game like a boy instead of using a rifle like a man.

Sure, I knew I wasn't a man, but I had nothing against hurrying up the process all I could. And we needed help because there was less and less food right along. Times were hard, as people said. It wasn't a new rifle which explains how Pa could afford it. It was a single shot Remington, and I had to use my pocket knife to pry out the empty shells once I'd shot them, but it was mine. I'd just have to be a good shot with it— there wouldn't be any second chances. But now with a rifle I could shoot game farther away than with a slingshot. Now I might be able to shoot some jackrabbits and sell them in town for the bounty. We never ate jackrabbits: Ma said they were bound to be tough, and they probably carried diseases.

Pa had already told me long ago about not hunting animals in the spring. That's the time they're bearing their young and it's too easy to shoot a doe and cause a bunch of little ones to starve to death. Worse is shooting one that's pregnant. I knew better than to try hunting rabbits in February or March, but in the early summer and on into fall and winter, I'd be bringing home young cottontails for our dinner table, and Ma and Pa would both be proud of me.

We were sitting at the breakfast table on a Saturday morning that year, May 1936 it was, when Pa announced, "There's a rabbit drive tomorrow, Ben. I thought you and I would go."

"What's a rabbit drive, Pa?" I asked.

"Can I go, too?" Billy asked.

"The rabbits have been eating too much of the wheat. A bunch of the farmers have decided we have to do something about it."

"Can I, Pa?" Billy repeated.

"No."

I could feel Ma silent, not saying anything in a way that left the air heavy. Rachel ate quietly.

I tried again, "How does it work?"

"You'll see," he answered, and I knew I wasn't to ask again. Pa never used more words than he needed, and other farmers were the same. They could engage in an hour-long conversation made up entirely of monosyllables.

This reticence to avoid using too many words just naturally carried over into everything that they did. My father and all the other men I knew when I was growing up distrusted anyone who dealt in words. They were handicapped by their lack of education and self-conscious about it, so they distrusted anybody who used words too easily. Words were too valuable to be used freely: a man needed to be sparing of what he said. It was like talking about love.

Anybody who came right out and used a word like love when referring to other people had to be either a minister or somebody who had no sense of privacy. I guess to most men of those days talking of love was about the same thing as swearing or sex: if you have to do it, get it over with quickly and out of hearing of the kids.

A joke I've heard since growing up says that the people of the midwest and the central plains don't talk much, and when they do they hardly open their mouths because they're afraid of the dust or the sand getting in. I think maybe the men of that time had too great a dose of dignity. To my father and men like him, life was circumscribed by many rules of conduct which even though they were unwritten were to be observed nonetheless. A man who talked too much about himself or his wife or his children was suspect: he probably had something to hide.

I'd watch and listen as Raymond Swain bragged about how much wheat he had harvested, or how much more it had rained at his place than anybody else's, or how well his wife's sister was doing in St. Louis. The men would sit there along the wall of the pool hall with the chairs tilted back, or they'd hunch over the domino or card table, under their caps, concentrating on their game and answer only occasionally, "Ayup." "'S that so?" "Well—" But occasionally I'd catch their covert looks to each other as Raymond Swain bragged on, striding about among them like an orator of days gone by, and after he'd leave there'd be a comment or two. "Well, he sure likes to talk, don't he?"

"Ayup. Too bad he can't run for congress."

It was not dignified for a man to talk the way Raymond Swain did, and I'd have been mortally embarrassed had he been my father, but I wonder if he ever told Roberta, his wife, or his kids, Jimmy, Susie, or even Tommy who was my age, that he loved them? Raymond Swain didn't seem like a real farmer to me.

After breakfast I saw my father empty the rain gauge of dust, maybe hoping that the next time it would be water that he could pour out. Most of the times those years, however, the gauge registered only dirt. One of the stores in town had a hand-printed sign placed in the window: "Free land. Bring your own container." That had seemed funny at first, but in time, it got to be a nagging reminder of the transience of our lives when even the land beneath our feet was always shifting and blowing. Back in those days we didn't just work the land, we breathed it; it was impossible not to.

Closed by drought and depression (National Archives)

There were some chores to do around the place that morning which I had to help with, being twelve and almost a man, but in the afternoon Billy and I took the rifle and went away from the house, looking for a rabbit or anything else for food. It was near the end of May now, and there was no danger of shooting a doe with babies. The young cottontails would be getting big enough to eat while still tender.

When we had money in those days, we'd have a small piece of pot roast or meat loaf made from hamburger, 2 or 3 pounds. Otherwise, unless we could get something hunting, there was no meat on our table.

The big meal of the week back then was Sunday dinner. Dinner was at 12:30 or 1:00, and it was the high point of the week for all of us kids, maybe for Ma and Pa, too. In those days we appreciated food a great deal more when we had it because so many times we didn't. Sunday dinner would be meat loaf, if we could afford to buy the hamburger, with mashed potatoes and gravy, and canned corn or peas. If Ma had time, there might be a pie or cake, too, but that wasn't often. Ma worked all the time, but I heard her say more than once, "I never seem to get caught up."

It was a dispiriting life for her. Looking back I can see why she wouldn't have wanted to bake fresh bread or anything else in the oven, especially when stove wood was scarce. This was before we got electricity or before anybody had natural gas, so timing whatever was baking was a matter of watching pretty close to make sure it didn't burn. We ate store-bought bread more than once.

Rachel, Billy, and I didn't like church much, what with having to kneel for most of the service on hard, unpadded kneeling rails. The service, in Latin, lasted an hour or more. I was always relieved to be released once again into the land of the living after Sunday morning Mass, and Sunday dinner made the release all the more welcome.

Other meals weren't as pleasant. Many times we had boiled potatoes in their jackets, as Ma would say. This was when she was too tired to peel them. If there was bread, then we could make a sandwich, maybe, using apple butter or peanut butter or home-made jelly.

Eating lunch at school was always an embarrassment because other kids wanted to know what we had. There were days when we had only cold pancakes left over from breakfast, and we were ashamed to let the town kids know we had so little.

Rachel and Billy and I would go off by ourselves away from the others to eat usually, forming our own little closed society. For the same reason I never stayed overnight at anybody else's house. I wanted to, but it was impossible to have somebody come to our house to stay because we were too poor and we had no place for him. Maybe Pa's dignity was a legacy to all of us, but we were frighteningly aware that we were poor and dirty.

When I was a boy, I had only a partial notion of how closely poverty is tied to filth, but I know now that they always go hand in hand. It is simply impossible to be clean while being poor. Even Miss Lehrer didn't understand this completely; I remember her saying things like, "There's nothing wrong with hand-me-down clothes, or patches, so long as they're clean."

How could they be clean? We had no washing machine; we had Ma's wash kettle, the wash board, and a stove to heat water on. I'd heard of people washing their clothes in a creek or a river, but the draw that ran through the pasture had dried up long ago. To wash clothes took all day. We had to start heating water on the cookstove early in the morning, pouring hot water into the kettle and heating more water until finally about noon, maybe it was hot enough. Then we had to scrub the clothes on the washboard with home-made soap which wasn't nearly as good as what's advertised on television today. Then the clothes had to be hung up on the makeshift line Pa had strung up. While they were hanging out, another dust storm might come through, and that meant starting all over again. After they were dry, they had to be put away or ironed which was, itself, another big job. We had no real cupboards, so it was just natural that everything became dirty. Clothes lying here and there are hard to keep separated into stacks of clean and dirty: eventually everything becomes dirty.

Keeping oneself clean was only a little easier than washing the clothes. Since it didn't require as much water, the heating took a shorter time, but there still had to be a good supply of kindling and wood for the stove. Privacy was also not a simple matter. I guess most people used a sheet hung over a line or the backs of chairs, or they ignored privacy entirely. In our family when we took baths on Saturday night we were very careful about not intruding on someone else's bath, Billy was first to use the water, followed by Rachel and me. Then last, after we had gone to bed, would be Ma and Pa. By then the water was cloudy with dirt and soap, but I remember even that was refreshing.

The worst of all—worse than being poor, hungry, dirty, cold with improper or inadequate clothing, worse even than being shunned by so-called Christians—was the degradation we all endured. It was as if we had been marked as outcasts. Sociologists write today that America is a classless society. This is hardly any truer today than it was in the thirties. But I know for certain it was a lie then. As farmers we ranked below people who lived in town. As sharecroppers we ranked below true land-owners. And as Catholics we ranked below Protestants.

All of this eroded our dignity just as the wind eroded our wheat fields. Dignity is a delicate quality; the wrong word spoken out of misguided good intentions can reduce a child to little more than chagrin at being alive. I have to refer to my memories to fully understand how much pain it caused Ma and Pa to accept clothing for us kids when we needed it. Of course, the need wasn't the issue: nearly everybody needed things. But I see their faces now as they were made to crawl for things their children needed. Once the Red Cross distributed food and clothing, but Ma refused to accept anything. "That's for the poor people," she said, ignoring that we didn't always have milk and bread or decent clothing or shoes.

Ma and Pa remained impassive through it all, but I remember the muffled sounds of my mother crying late at night when she should have been resting for the next interminable day, and I remember hearing no sounds from Pa.

Maybe he had no comfort left in him to offer to her or to anyone else. Poverty isolates people from society and it can force them to isolate themselves from each other, even their loved ones.

Everybody who has lived through childhood knows the cruelty of children. Like baby chicks, they look for the vulnerable spots—the flecks of red—and when they find them, they peck like cannibals. When we had been able to afford it, we had raised baby chicks, about the time Billy was born, and it had been my job to watch over them. As soon as I saw one with a spot of blood, I had to catch it and smear the spot with axle grease. Then the chicks would leave that one alone.

What was needed was people grease. After times got so hard, there was no way to smear our vulnerable spots over with grease. There <u>was</u> no people grease, and even if there had been we couldn't have paid for it.

Only the farm boys wore overalls. I hated them because they identified me as someone who was stupid and dirty. Not one single boy from town had to wear overalls. But they were economical, and when my father bought clothes, Billy and I got overalls. Shoes were another matter. I think I was almost a grown man before I got my first pair of new shoes that actually fit my feet instead of somebody else's.

I know Miss Lehrer saw the difference in class represented in our school. She couldn't have missed that the boys in the overalls always kept to themselves. Sometimes I think it might have been easier for the girls, but then I remember Vernon Jones picking on Rachel and calling her "Dirty cat-lick" until I had to fight him. He was in the eighth grade, and I was only in the seventh, but there wasn't anything else I could do. He left us alone after that, but he and his sister, Sue Ann who was in my grade, always acted so special—so privileged—that I'd get a sick feeling in my stomach if I was near them too long. It got so that when Pa went into their store, I'd wait outside for him. It was only a little crossroads store with general merchandise, but you'd have thought it was Macy's in New York the way they acted about it. To us they were rich, and to them we were poor, and the two never came together.

Miss Lehrer acted ignorant of all of that in school. She worked hard to give us tips on keeping clean and taking care of clothing, but most of us couldn't even try the things she suggested. When she talked about three balanced meals a day, there were very few of us in the room who had any first-hand experience of what that meant.

Sometimes it all runs together now, becoming one big impression. Sitting here in a well-lighted room at a comfortable desk, wearing comfortable clothing that fits, and enjoying the satisfying feeling of a meal digesting, it's hard to recapture the essence of it, even to myself, let alone try to make it plain to people who have been watching television since birth.

I'm seventy-seven, and I'm retired, and I remember our first radio. It was an imposing piece of furniture that announced its presence in the room just by being there, about the way these giant television sets do today. Ma and Pa got it a couple of years after I was born, and we'd listen to it of a night for news of the outside world when the battery was fresh. The battery was good for about six months before it had to be recharged. Sometimes, if Pa felt like it, we'd play cards: easy games like rummy, crazy 8, Old Maid, hearts, and five-point pitch. He even showed me the rudiments of poker despite Ma's disapproval. We used matches from the big five-cent box to bet with.

How can I explain to children nurtured on neon lights that kerosene lamps were what we saw by? To someone who loves to read, the coming of electricity and the electric light was an illumination of the mind. It was my job to keep the chimneys of the lamps wiped clean with newspaper, and I had to make sure there was enough kerosene, or coal oil as we called it, in the base to keep the lamp burning. People in town had electricity, and some even had indoor plumbing, but none of the farmers or sharecroppers did.

Going to the outhouse after dark in those days was not only unpleasant, it could also be hazardous. We had no flashlights, and the outdoors at night always seemed more ominous to me when I had to go to the outhouse than at any other time. But we did what we had to do. People joke about the outhouse nowadays and the Sears Roebuck catalogues, but it wasn't something we laughed over then.

As our way to the pasture led past the outhouse, Billy and I walked past it on our way. I was carrying my rifle, hoping to find some game or a jackrabbit to shoot for the bounty. "Ben, can I carry the rifle?"

"Sure, Billy. Just be careful with it. And when I say I need it, you hand it over immediately."

"Okay, Ben."   He took the rifle, reverently, and I remembered how I had been at six, wishing for a rifle of my own. If anyone had told me then that it would be six years before I got one, I'd have cried out in disappointment and grief. "Gee, this is a nice rifle, Ben. Do you suppose maybe Pa might give me one some day?"

"Sure, Billy. Or maybe if I can earn enough money with jackrabbits and such, I can buy a new one. Then you could have this one."

Billy studied me to make sure I wasn't teasing him. He wanted to believe me, but he didn't want to be disappointed.

"Maybe Ma wouldn't want me to have it," he said in a small voice.

"Yeah, maybe. We'll see later on."

Sometimes it seemed that there was a whole generation separating Billy and me. Those six years were an unbridgeable gulf at times, but at other times he was my best friend. He always looked up to me, and I always looked after him. He had friends at school, I knew, and they had their games they played, but he always went along with me if I asked him.

When we got to the pasture, we saw the cow and calf standing in one corner, so we walked in the opposite direction, not hurrying, just paying attention to the grass which was trying to grow but having to fight for every bit of moisture.

Bessie had been a good cow, but her last calf, born in February, wasn't as strong as earlier ones, and she, too, wasn't doing well. There was hardly enough milk for the calf, so we no longer went through the pretense of milking her.

In later years when I told people I had come from a farm, they were envious of the life I must have had growing up: fresh milk, fresh-baked bread, fresh vegetables from the garden, and the clean outdoors to live and work in. Many times I didn't bother to try to set them straight, but most mornings when I was a boy I went to school without having drunk a glass of milk: there wasn't any.

We walked down into the draw which I remembered had run full with rain water in other springs, but this year it had been nearly dry; now it was overgrown with weeds. I suppose every farm kid has asked the question many times over, but I never have understood and still don't to this day why weeds continue to grow when there isn't enough moisture for crops.

The garden was on the other side of the draw, beside the windmill. Even it appeared hopeless. What few carrots, potatoes, and radishes were visible were hardly worth keeping the animals out. The tomato plants stood forlornly, rejecting our hopes of fresh fruit later in the summer. We had worked hard in the garden, but to keep it up despite the drought and dust was almost impossible.

I had Billy lean the rifle against the windmill while I released the brake on the blades above. It creaked in the wind as the fan swung around away from the wind and the blades began racing around.

Boise City, Oklahoma farm (Lange, Library of Congress)

The water came up from far below, cool and fresh, and spilled out of the spout where Billy and I took turns catching it in the pail and watering the plants. Pa had said we should let the garden die as water was too scarce; if the well at the house went dry, we'd have to carry water from this well, but I didn't want to give up on the garden yet. Billy was of an age that he usually accepted everything I said, so he didn't argue.

We poured water over the plants, washing off the dust momentarily, but that wouldn't last long. They'd soon be bathed in dust again. When we finished, we each took a drink before walking on toward the northwest corner of the pasture.

If the wind had stopped so the dust could settle, or if it had rained to wash the air clean, it would have been a beautiful day. I remember days when I was younger that the air was alive with the sounds of meadowlarks singing their repetitive melodies which I answered by whistling, and the insects buzzed alongside the road, and everything was clean, fresh, and green. The sky was a giant blue arena overhead with great, fluffy cumulus clouds floating against that impressive backdrop, occasionally cutting off the sunshine. On those days I lay on my back with Jyp, our dog beside me, and looked for pictures in the clouds.

We got Jyp just before I started to school. He just wandered in off the road one day and stayed. When times got bad, however, we couldn't afford to feed him. After he started eating eggs, I didn't see him again. I guess he could have wandered off, but I imagine Pa killed him. A farm dog that eats eggs is worthless. I knew that, but I still missed him. And I think it would have been good for Rachel and Billy to have a dog, too. We had three cats that lived in the barn, but they were almost wild, living off the mice they caught themselves. When one had kittens, Ma made me drown them as there wasn't anything for them to live on. I cried as I did it, but it was my job. They didn't stay up very long in the water, and it was pitiful having to pick them out and then bury them.

Donald J. Richardson

As we walked through the pasture, we kicked up little puffs of dust along the way which the wind carried along with us. Most of the buffalo grass was down to its roots. About the only plants that looked good were the prickly pear cactus, but even they were covered with dust.

Windmill and stock watering hole

(Rothstein, Library of Congress)

Suddenly, something exploded ahead of us and ran off to the right; it was a jack rabbit. I reached for the rifle which Billy was holding out. The jack was about fifty yards away, but I had practiced and I might be able to get him. I squeezed the trigger and saw him jump a bit, but then he sat back down.

"You got him, Ben!" Billy cried. "You got him!"

"I only winged him," I said. Quickly I pried out the used shell and dropped in another. The jack was still sitting there, almost as if he were posing for a picture. With the second shot he fell over.

Billy ran ahead to pick him up and carry him back to me. "He's a big one," he announced. I put the rabbit into the game bag I had fashioned out of a gunny sack and threw it over my shoulder. "I could carry him, Ben," Billy offered, so I let him carry the sack. When I got to town, I would sell the jackrabbit at the produce station where people also sold cream and eggs.

Mr. Herrmann bought animal skins and jackrabbits, too. He paid five cents each for the jackrabbits which would help to pay for my rifle shells.

After I had reloaded the rifle, we walked on following the draw up toward the northwest corner of the pasture.

One spring the draw had overflowed its banks and flooded part of the pasture. There had even been some fish in the water which became stranded after the water went down. When I saw them, I waded into the pool and caught them bare-handed. We had fried fish for supper that night.

As we got to the corner of the pasture, I slowed down because I knew there might be a cottontail or two in the fence rows. The wind piled up the tumbleweeds against the fences, and the rabbits used the tumbleweeds as shelters.

Stuck in dust (National Archives)

One of the farmers in our neighborhood didn't have fence rows around his wheat. Unlike the other farmers, he farmed right up to the edge of the field, so that where the road stopped his field started. Not only that, he cut all the weeds beside the road and kept them plowed under. His fields were as neat as a mathematics design with no tumbleweeds hanging in the fences and no fence rows for animals to hide in. Only years later did I realize that this was wrong. Even rabbits have to live somewhere.

As we neared the corner, three cottontails suddenly jumped up and ran, two in the same direction. I sighted along the rifle after them, waiting for them to stop to look back which they did after getting about thirty yards away. Then I shot the one nearest us. The other one jumped and ran. After waiting to be sure I wouldn't shoot again, Billy squeezed through the barbed wire fence and ran to get the rabbit.

"He's a nice one, Ben," he said with a smile. "He'll be good for supper tonight."

"I'd like to get some more to go with him," I answered.

After we added the cottontail to the jackrabbit in the gunny sack, we headed east along the fence row, walking cautiously and slowly. Soon another jackrabbit bounded away. He didn't stop in range, so I didn't shoot. If I had had a rifle with an ejector that worked, I could try a running shot, but with only a single shot, I hated to risk it. Then another cottontail ran away from us to the east, stopping after he got behind a stone post.

Because wooden posts cost more than stone posts, many fences in western Kansas are built with native limestone. I've helped Pa repair fence, and it's a big job even for a man, let alone for a kid to shove those two- or three-hundred-pound posts around. Since I've grown up, I've learned that there's an art to cutting the posts out of limestone, but at the time I didn't appreciate that. Stone posts were just something we used and part of our lives. In fact, nowadays there are even museums for post rock and various strands of barbed wire. How we'd have laughed about that in those days. We never saw those posts in romantic terms but as work. And barbed wire was something you took your chances with only when necessary.

Instead of walking straight east, I angled south so that I could shoot the rabbit as he sat on the east side of the post. When I got in range, I could make out his head as he cocked it, listening. Then I squeezed the trigger, and he jumped up and fell over.

"Good shot, Ben," Billy cried, running to pick up the rabbit. "Now we'll have plenty for tonight."

"Yes, but maybe we'll get another before we go back. Then you can help me skin them."

After I shot a third cottontail along the fence row, we headed for the house, Billy carrying the rifle and I the game bag.

There was an old rickety table beside the house which I used to clean game on. First, I skinned the cottontails, being careful not to damage the skins, and then Billy held the back legs up as I opened up the body and removed the entrails.

The cats would eat most of what we didn't. We saved the skins for drying and tanning, and then I cut up the meat into frying-sized pieces which I put into a dish pan and took to the pump to wash off while Billy pumped water over them. Then we took the meat into the kitchen to give to Ma.

"I got three cottontails, Ma," I said as I put the dishpan down on the table.

Ma was sitting at the table mending socks. She looked up and smiled faintly, "That's fine, Ben. I'll fry some for supper tonight, and the rest we can have tomorrow night. Unless you think you might be tired of fried rabbit."

I shook my head at Ma's little joke. "We never get tired of fried rabbit, right, Billy? "

"No, Sir!"

"Is Pa at home?"

"No, he went into town to see about some things."

"Ma, do you know what a rabbit drive is?"

"Yes, Ben."

"Well, I don't know why Pa won't tell me what it is."

"I imagine he wants you to see for yourself, Ben."

Billy spoke from the water pail where he was getting a drink. "I don't see why I can't go, too."

"It's no place for children," Ma answered.

I began to wonder then just what was wrong with a rabbit drive if it wasn't any place Billy could go. But Ma wasn't going to tell me, so I might as well not ask again.

After the evening chores were finished, I stood and watched the sunset. In addition to the unpleasant grittiness the dust caused in our lives, it also yielded beauty. I remember sunsets which were suitable for framing with the best photographs ever shown in <u>National</u> <u>Geographic</u>. Few people talked about them, maybe because they didn't even see them. People get so involved in making a living, especially farmers, that they go through life without even noticing the green of a field of wheat or the gold of a piece of wheat straw. The sunsets were spectacular productions mounted for our entertainment, but most people ignored them.

For supper that night we had the fried rabbit, with mashed potatoes and gravy and fresh corn bread that Ma baked. I've had many different kinds of meat in my life, but fresh fried cottontail is one of the best. We'd have a pheasant or two, occasionally, when I caught them sitting, and we ate some of the wild pigeons from the cupola of the barn when I could catch them, but fried rabbit was always my favorite. Maybe that was because I felt more like the provider of the meal.

I know that when I got my first full-time, regular job as an adult, there was a special feeling in getting a paycheck that I had earned all by myself. Anything bought with it became special, too. Later on that feeling is lost, but at first it's like a new world of self-reliance opening up to show us that we can do just about anything.

Pa had brought home Hersey's chocolate bars with almonds in them, one for each of us. It was a game with Rachel and Billy to try to discover which Hersey's bar had the most almonds before opening the wrapper. They would feel along the backs of the bars and count the almonds. Most of them had five, but occasionally there would be one with six, and I've seen them with seven, too. I suppose that was to make up for the ones that had only four. Those always seemed unfair.

After eating the chocolate, they carefully refolded the paper and slipped it back inside the outer wrapper to try to fool each other that there was still chocolate inside.

We usually had hard candy for Christmas, so there was no shortage of sweets. Hershey's bars, on the other hand, were so rare in our lives that they were a treat. Pa must have won at playing pitch.

After supper, Rachel and I washed the dishes while Billy brought in wood to fill the wood box beside the cook stove. We had an Imperial range which nowadays is an antique. In fact, everything we owned back then is an antique today.

That's ironic, but that doesn't make it any easier in my memory. The ice box was an antique, but knowing that didn't provide money to buy ice for it. Most families got along from day to day without such luxuries as refrigerators and running water.

The cook stove, or range, had a reservoir which a person could fill with water before cooking; then after the meal was cooked, there was hot water. That probably was very handy when the stove was new. Unfortunately, ours was old, and the reservoir had long ago rusted through. To get hot water, we had to heat it on top of the stove.

I don't remember when it started, but Rachel and I developed a routine out of washing dishes which made it less a chore than a recreation. Nobody we knew at school liked to wash dishes; usually it was the girls' job, so I didn't tell anybody I helped, but for me at least, and I think for Rachel, too, it was a time to help someone else and to cooperate. While we washed and dried, we sang. I sang the melody and she the harmony on "K-K-Katy," or "The Band Played On," and the job never seemed oppressive or burdensome as it did when a person did it by himself.

I'm not saying we understood or appreciated it all at that time; probably we didn't. But as I replay the tape in my head, I see us standing there washing, rinsing, and drying those dishes as if we loved each other. I guess we did, but we never said it.

The three years' difference between Rachel and me at those times seemed very small. Usually, I saw her as one of the little kids who were very bothersome to someone who was almost grown up, almost a teenager anyway. But when we stood there after supper and did the dishes, we became a team.

I think everyone else in the family felt it, too. Pa would usually find something to do in the kitchen, even if it was only loading his pipe with Prince Albert tobacco from the tin he carried in his overalls bib pocket next to his pocket watch. He'd tamp the tobacco in carefully and then deliberately strike a kitchen match to hold over the bowl, getting the tobacco to burn evenly and steadily. Then he might read a newspaper or a farm magazine if there had been any left on the free table at church.

Ma sat at the table, trying to do mending in the bad light. She wore those cheap eyeglasses that were sold in bulk at F. W.

Woolworth's, what we called the dime store. I think she never ever had a set of prescription glasses all her life.

Billy raced in and out, hurrying to fill the wood box and even offering to help with the dishes. At those times in our lives there was harmony, not only the harmony of the music Rachel and I made, but the harmony of working together and being together as a family, a group of people who needed and depended on each other.

"Sing 'She'll Be Comin' 'Round the Mountain When She Comes,'" Billy asked the first chance he got. It was his favorite song because he was just getting to where he could remember the verses, and he liked to sing, too. Then would come "Old MacDonald" which had been his first favorite.

I remember singing along with the radio in those days, too, but it wasn't the same as singing in the family. When we all sang together, we held the drought, the debtors, and the dust storms at bay.

Oh, they were out there all right, beating at our little shack trying to get in and wreck what little comfort we had, but when we sang they were less important. Maybe for a moment while our voices chimed together, we forgot that we rarely knew what we'd have to eat tomorrow.

As I look back on my life then and consider the life I've lived since leaving the dust of that Kansas farm, I see that music has been an important force in it. I was lucky to be allowed to work my way through college, and after that I had people help me, too, so after I left that farm I think I never really wanted for things the way we did then. But no matter what I was doing, whether it was going to college—getting up in the dark to work before classes started and staying up late at night to study—or working a full-time job and supporting a family of my own, I always made time to sing. Sometimes it was only the church choir, but even then the magic of music always seemed to lift me up and away from life's daily irritations.

In a way music spoiled me for regular church-going because the times I've gone to church and not sung in the choir have always disappointed me. The service always seemed incomplete if I couldn't raise my voice in praise. Perhaps it was a way of giving back what little I could, but I've always felt that if they let me sing in the choir, I had to support the church. Maybe singing is just a way of my holding on to that modest bit of happiness that we created those evenings in our kitchen when we sang.

I suppose it's because of those evenings, too, that I've never disliked washing dishes. When I worked in the Corner Grill Cafe after I left home, washing dishes, it was a job nobody else wanted. Even the waitresses had better jobs. But I was restoring balance to life by making things clean all over again, and when I got finished, my own hands would be clean, not as they were when I worked in the service station later on: impossible to get the grime out.

Maybe that's why I don't like automatic dishwashers, too. Perhaps I'm simply remembering the music of our voices and compared to that the noise of the machine is not worth abiding for the results; it disrupts and irritates.

After we finished the dishes, it was time for our weekly baths. Sometimes in the winter months, we'd skip that routine because of the cold and the discomfort, but now half-way through May, it was easier. We had started water re-heating as soon as we poured it out for the dishes. There was Saturday night music playing from the radio in the background as we each took our turns and then crawled into bed. Mass was at

9:00 Sunday morning, so we needed to get to sleep. People's ideas of bedtime differed a great deal back then from today. There was a respect bordering on reverence for being in bed by ten o'clock. Nowadays the ten o'clock news on television keeps people up until 10:30, and other things that never would have been allowed to interfere back then keep people up until after midnight and beyond.

I remember staying up past ten o'clock only for Midnight Mass on Christmas Eve. There must have been other times, too, but they don't occur to me. What did we sacrifice as we gave up those inflexible rules of conduct for our daily lives? With maturity and adulthood came the freedom to stay up all night if a person wanted, and I've done that, too, but in practice it's often less desirable than anticipated.

One August night, years later, I worked all night helping tear down a carnival because the workers were promised fifty cents an hour, and it was money I needed. When I saw the sun come up in the east, it wasn't nearly as impressive as it should have been, even when it wiped away the total blackness of the night. Then I felt doubly cheated when I got paid only twenty-five cents an hour. Having no contract, I took the twenty-five cents.

At other times in my life, after I discovered the true importance of books, I stayed up all night reading, until the edges of night's cover were eased back by dawn. Then I'd slip guiltily into bed.

At twelve I was still reading books for boys—books by Robert Louis Stevenson, Sir Walter Scott, and Mark Twain—books that I could dive into like a pool of water with nothing on its surface—clean, clear, and enticing—tempting me beyond what I could possibly resist. Later on I fell into that bottomless pit of information and education that can drown a person when he jumps in unheeding as I did. I'd read as fast as I could, trying to finish the book, trying to assimilate everything available before it escaped me. In those years I read as if fear or fever drove me, in great gulps of print. Since then I've slowed down, but there's still some of the magic in reading at discovering a personality hidden in a book, the lure of the unknown which calls to me like a siren of insatiable desire.

During the night the wind came up so that on Sunday morning, the dust in the air was worse.

April 14, 1935—Black Sunday in Western Kansas

(Kansas State Historical Society)

We made our brave attempts at getting ready for Mass, washing our faces and necks and ears, and putting on clean clothes. We had no Sunday clothes or best clothes then, only some that were less patched and ragged than others. Rich people say there's no dishonor in wearing patched clothes, but I think that's because when they do it they do it out of choice. Poor people would just as soon have clothing that is whole and unpatched.

As we climbed into the Model T, the wind died down and, by the time we reached St. Joseph's in town, it was calm. The dust had begun to settle out of the air onto everything like powdered sugar dusted over Christmas cookies. Ma and Rachel held handkerchiefs in front of their faces, and Billy and I kept our mouths covered, too, but it was impossible not to breathe it in. Nowadays, people are very concerned with emphysema and other diseases of the lungs caused by smoking. I wonder how much our health deteriorated in those days as a result of breathing so much dust? There was no such thing as a clean handkerchief back then. We blew and spit mud up from our lungs, throats, and mouths.

Sunday Mass was the same as always. The Catholic religion in those days didn't kow-tow to children's need to be entertained: religion wasn't <u>meant</u> to be entertaining. After I had done my duty by saying the rosary, I let my mind drift, trying to ignore the pain in my knees. Father Lewkowitz made several announcements before saying that a funeral would be held tomorrow for Isaiah Jacobs, a farmer who had lived in the county most of his life after emigrating from Europe. The wake was to be that evening at the church.

As Father Lewkowitz gave his sermon, I wondered what life had been for Isaiah Jacobs. He had been sixty-seven when he died, Father said, and he left behind seven sons and four daughters. Even for those days, that was a large family. I imagined that for him to come to America had been a giant step. Did he have as much trouble with English as the other immigrants did?

I'm ashamed to remember it now, but I comforted myself that at least I was an American, not one of those Roosians, as we pronounced it in those days. Many of the people in our area had emigrated from the Ukraine and Eastern Europe, and naturally they brought their languages and customs with them. For those of us who spoke only English at home, they were truly foreign.

At school, we made fun of the kids who couldn't speak English. Instead of helping them to learn to become Americans, we made it harder for them, teasing and ridiculing them, thus driving them back into their first culture.

Donald J. Richardson

Tenant farmer daughter (Rusinow, National Archives)

This need to raise oneself at another's expense, I suspect, is almost universal. But the sad part of that time of my life is that while I felt put upon at being called names for being poor, dirty, a share-cropper, and a Catholic, I didn't hesitate at calling other people names because they carried onions in their lunch bags and ate them as we did apples. Any difference that we could use to raise ourselves, we did. I guess it's partially learned from adults, as I'd heard my father and others say disparaging things about the German or Russian immigrants, but more important, I believe, is the inner sense of being incomplete or unfulfilled. That self-doubt is quite difficult to resolve as it doesn't go away. One way to hide it, however, is to point a finger at somebody else and say, "He's worse than I am. Look at him!" This deflects the spotlight and momentarily saves us. Yet, it's a salvation bought by debasing the human spirit.

Then I thought about Isaiah Jacobs lying in his coffin. Surely the dust would filter in there, too; death could hardly be dust-proof any more than our lives were. They would keep him covered as long as possible, naturally, but at the wake they would open up the coffin. How could they clean the dust off him? Or would they want to? Why even bother? "Ashes to ashes and dust to dust" is what reminds us of where we begin and end up. Maybe this was some joke that I couldn't understand, mixing the dust in with the body and burying the whole mess. Is this what our lives were to come to finally, just a little snicker of relief, dust in the wind?

After I started college I read "Hamlet" and learned that I wasn't the only one who thought of such things. Hamlet himself was aware that there was something more going on that went beyond the skull he held up which had once been his friend and servant, Yorick. But when I was twelve, there was no relief for such questions. Ma and Pa would have had no patience for them, even if I could have asked them, and there was no one I felt at ease enough to ask. Miss Lehrer might know, but I'd have been mortified to open myself up to her that much.

Having read many books in my life, I have concluded that one characteristic that separates men is the ability to see oneself as removed from the mainstream, apart from everyone else. Most people are quite un-self-conscious, seeing themselves only when they look into a mirror or chance upon a reflected image on the surface of a pool of water or momentarily in somebody else's eyes. But people who ask questions do not settle for this lack of awareness.

Questions cry out in the night, and they are not answered by the mouthed pieties of religion or the momentary comfort of a parent's soothing hand. Up to a certain age, a person is willing to be reassured, but when he begins to explore the confines of his world and of his brain, he subjects everything to the same unrelenting inspection, and when he lives among unquestioning, unperceptive people, he becomes alien, partially out of choice.

At the time the thought didn't occur to me, but now I wonder: could Isaiah Jacobs have had that same questioning bent? The thought at twelve years of age would have horrified me, for I had no wish to ally myself with an Isaiah Jacobs or any other "Roosian." But why not? What was to keep a man who had fathered eleven children from questioning why? Life's obligations aren't all that we think about, even though they do take up most of our time. Because he thought in a different language, was he unqualified to think abstract thoughts?

As a twelve-year-old can, I shrugged off Isaiah Jacobs and death when Mass ended. When I had to face them again, I would.

The day was nearly beautiful when we emerged from the church. There was no wind, and the sun shone brightly, almost in forgiveness. Except for the layer of dust, one would never suspect what we had come through. The future held promise once again.

Driving home, I looked back and saw the great cloud of dust that we pulled behind us, like tin cans trailing behind a newly-married couple's car, only silent and ominous.

When we reached home, Pa said, "Ben, you and Billy check on the wood pile. It's getting low."

"Okay, Pa," I answered.

After we changed clothes, Billy and I went out to the stump where we split chunks of wood and chopped up kindling. The stump had been left there purposely as a chopping block. The axe had left the top of it riddled with deep clefts, but it still served as a type of work table. We would place a block of wood on top of the stump and then try to split it into pieces small enough to fit into the cook stove or the heating stove in winter. We had a sledge hammer and one iron wedge which often became stuck in a crack; then we'd have to use wooden blocks to finish the job.

The good axe was double-bladed which meant one could use one blade until it got dull and then switch to the other before having to sharpen it again. There was also a single-bladed axe which I called mine. It was less dangerous. When a person used it, he didn't have to always check to make sure there was no one standing behind him.

Billy and I took turns splitting blocks of already sawed lengths of logs. Pa and I had hauled the branches and trees up from the creek south of our farm. We tried always to take only the dead ones. Green wood doesn't burn well anyway, and a living tree is valuable in Kansas. Later on the government began paying for seedlings for farmers in Kansas to plant wind breaks, but in those days there were very few trees.

Splitting wood is hard work, so we were both relieved when Rachel called to us, "Dinner's ready."

After Pa said the blessing, we ate in silence mostly. I was looking forward to finding out about the rabbit drive. How could a person drive rabbits, I wondered. If they were anything like chickens, that would be impossible.

I had tried to drive the chickens into the chicken house during storms, and I knew that when they didn't want to go, they didn't. Chickens will fly right back at somebody who stands flapping his arms and crying "Shoo."

I also knew from hunting rabbits that they had a habit of circling back toward the hunter. What would happen then?

After dinner, Pa said, "Ben, you go out to the chicken house and get that roll of chicken wire and put it into the car."

"Okay, Pa," I answered. As I left the kitchen, I noticed Billy standing there, wanting to ask to be allowed to go again but knowing he wouldn't be permitted, so he didn't say anything.

As I carried the chicken wire to the car, I wondered how we would possibly make a pen for wild rabbits. How would we get them to go into it?

When Pa came out, I asked, "Won't I need my rifle?"

"No" was all he said.

Then Pa and I got into the car and drove back toward town. When we got about three miles from town, I noticed there were more cars on the road, stirring up dust and all apparently going to the same place. When Pa parked the car along side the road,

I saw that there were cars and men and boys all along the road. Some had chicken wire as we did, and many were carrying sticks of wood or clubs. What were they for?

"Pa?"

"Just pay attention and follow directions, Ben." He didn't sound normal to me; it was almost as if he was comforting me after I had broken a bone or something bad had happened.

It was obvious that there was some sort of plan because everyone was spaced out alongside the road. I expected there would be talking and joking, but it was eerily quiet, almost like a funeral.

Then after some signal that I didn't see, we all began walking across a field in the same direction, like an army invading a foreign land, only this was an army of farmers and their sons in tattered clothing, carrying chicken wire and clubs.

I still didn't understand how it worked; what would make the rabbits stand still for us to catch them? And what would we do with them after we had them? Nobody had brought a rifle or a shotgun. It didn't make sense.

Pa and I were stationed about the middle of the line as we walked west. Ahead of us we could see an occasional cottontail or jackrabbit as it ran to escape. I didn't pay close attention to how far we walked or how long it took, but gradually I became aware of a rising pitch of excitement. What little talk there had been was gone now, but it had been replaced by something that felt like electricity in the air. The pace didn't seem to increase; when we started it had been the pace of the slowest or littlest boys, some no older than Billy, but now it seemed we must be getting nearer to where we were going and there seemed some great attraction in the air, like a giant magnet pulling us all on to the end.

When I realized I was hearing sounds, I also knew I had been hearing them for several minutes, but I couldn't identify them. Advancing toward us and closing in on both sides of us, I could see other men and boys, but they walked silently just as we did. What I was hearing sounded like far-off cries of someone in distress. I couldn't make out the words, and the whole sense was jumbled. The sounds were cries of fear, only they didn't resemble anything I had ever heard before.

Without warning, the whole line stopped. As I looked around, I saw that the chicken wire was now being unrolled and stretched along the line in front of the men and boys. Pa took the roll from me and stretched it out until it reached the ends of other sections on the right and the left. Then the whole line began advancing again, walking more slowly now behind the chicken wire.

Suddenly, I realized the cries were being made by the rabbits. The four sides of the box we made were slowly closing in on the rabbits caught within its confines, and they knew it. It couldn't have been more than a hundred yards across now, and steadily the distance grew less.

The men at the ends of the lines walked faster to meet the ends of the next line and to eventually make a giant circle. In the middle of this fluid enclosure there was a roiling of dust and bodies much like the dust storms that afflicted our lives, yet this was caused not by nature but by us. From the mass of rabbits and dust in the middle came such a pitiful wailing, I thought no one could bear it for long, yet we marched implacably on, no one saying anything, everyone evidently impervious to the terror and distress of those poor animals we were closing in on.

A jackrabbit drive (Kansas State Historical Society)

As we closed in, the pitch of activity in the circle became feverish. The rabbits were obviously frantic, yet there was no way for them to escape: in every direction was a fence with people behind it. What would we do if we were on the other side of the fence? Probably the same as the rabbits did. Some ran here and there, screaming frantically, hoping against hope for deliverance. Others sat quietly and trembled before their implacable fate, yet knowing they were doomed.

Maybe the rabbits didn't know; maybe rabbits don't sense and feel the same as human beings do. I hope this is so, but I doubt it because I watched as the men and boys began reaching over the fence with their clubs to kill the rabbits that were trying to escape, and the rabbits seemed to know that they were face to face with death. In this insanity of promiscuous violence they jumped up directly into the face of this army of death, some daring and challenging in a way that is totally opposed to the way rabbits normally behave. This, too, was terribly frightening.

As the circle closed, more and more of us had to take part in killing them. Pa was reaching over and swinging at those poor creatures, too, but it was all I could do to hold onto the fence and try to wait for this to be over. Maybe, I told myself, if I don't actually kill any of them, I won't be responsible, yet as I thought it I knew the gravity of the lie.

No one escaped that day, no rabbit and no man or boy who took part in it. Oh, yes, some rabbits did manage to slip underneath the fence and somehow get away, and some of us didn't swing a club so that the spattered blood didn't soil our clothes, but our souls were not clean.

I realized, too, as it was happening that some of the men were actually enjoying the experience. Maybe this was a cleansing experience for them, permitting them to release the terror and pity of their lives in a way that at least deflected it away from other people. But I was shocked and appalled. They might say it was just like hunting, but no hunter I've ever known hunted in such an obscene way.

The cries of the rabbits were high pitched and frightening, like a woman's scream only with less physical body to them.

When it was finally over and the last club had been brought down onto the last piece of living flesh, the silence was as much a confession as the rabbits' cries had been of alarm. There was no real joy in this hunt and no real satisfaction in its bounty.

The rabbits had to be picked up and loaded into pickups to be taken to town. Some would be eaten by our people; others would be shipped by train to people in Kansas City or St. Louis who needed food.

Hunters show some of the jack rabbits they shot during a rabbit roundup. The rabbits were sold for ten cents each, and the meat was shipped back east (Hutchinson News).

I rolled up our chicken wire and then stood silently, waiting for Pa to leave. Some of the men bent over for dust to rub onto the blood which had spattered their hands. They also rolled the clubs in the dust to obliterate the tell-tail signs. The dust would cover their hands now as after death it would cover their bodies, and their bodies, too, would become dust—dust to be blown about by the winds of life.

Some of the men picked out two or three of the cottontails to take home with them, to clean them and eat for supper or for tomorrow's meal. It was a great relief to me when Pa turned without taking any of the rabbits and began walking back toward our car.

Pa didn't say anything as we walked back to the car, across the dead field we had walked a short time before in company with other killers. Now, as we all straggled back to our parked vehicles, there was a little conversation, but it was subdued, even apologetic or embarrassed, as if I wasn't the only one who felt guilty.

After I put the roll of chicken wire into the back and sat in the passenger seat, Pa climbed behind the wheel and rolled a cigarette. He had often sent me to town to get tobacco and papers, so I knew that the Prince Albert was being rolled in Ritz-La papers; he wouldn't use any other kind.

When he finished, he struck a kitchen match and started the cigarette burning.

After he had puffed a moment, he said, "Something had to be done, Ben. They eat all the young wheat before it can get started." I didn't answer that. At the time I guess I didn't know what he was saying, but maybe he, too, felt how wrong it was. Shooting a cottontail with a single-shot rifle or a slingshot is an eternity apart from what we had just done. What we had done was immoral; I felt it then, and I know it now. It changed me, and I suppose in subtle ways it changed everybody who was there. Maybe the change wasn't apparent, as in my father, but that was the last rabbit drive he ever went on. There were more later on, but he never participated again.

What made this one more significant than earlier ones? Surely they had always been the same, with the end product identical. Why did this one make him quit? Was it my presence?

What did it do to the little kids who saw it, the ones Billy's age? Today kids wake from sleep screaming from nightmares as a result of television shows they've seen. Did this experience give those kids nightmares? I saw why Ma had said it was no place for someone Billy's age, and I was glad Pa had forbidden him to go. Why had he taken <u>me</u> along? I was twelve, almost a man, and perhaps it was time for me to face such realities.

However, I wished there had been a way someone could have forbidden all of us from taking part in it.

What did it do to the men who reveled in this orgy of killing? This was not the simple butchering of a pig or a steer, but murder on a scale only a psychopath could enjoy. Did it just reconfirm their values? Did it leave them essentially unchanged?

When we got home, I returned the chicken wire to the chicken house and went to do the evening chores. After I scattered grain for the chickens, I went to feed the pigs. We had a sow and several piglets which we hoped would give us one to butcher and the rest to sell.

As the pigs gobbled the mixture of wheat shorts mixed with water and table scraps, I leaned on the fence of their pen and wondered. Pa always warned us kids to stay out of the pig pen, especially when there were babies because the sow can be quite vicious. I tested that once by jumping into the pen and running across it; I jumped right out again when the sow chased me. We had heard horror stories of pigs being taken to market in the same wagon or truck with calves and when the animals got there the calves sometimes had no ears or even lips; the pigs had eaten them.

Are pigs governed primarily by their appetites? They eat nearly anything, from corn cobs to coal. In fact, the coal is said to be good for their systems. Not only that, they're nearly impossible to keep penned up. They dig and root with their noses until they get under the fence and escape. In order to prevent that, farmers clamp hog rings through their noses with a pair of pliers. It must hurt them as this keeps them from rooting so much. Where is the morality in the lives of pigs? Is there none?

When Billy asked me about the rabbit drive, I said it wasn't for little kids. "Well, what happened, Ben? Didn't you get any rabbits?"

"No," I answered, "I didn't."

That night for supper, Ma fried the rest of the cottontails I had shot the day before. When I realized what it was on the platter, I was no longer hungry. Pa didn't say anything to me, but I suppose he knew. I didn't eat cottontails for years after that, either. I'd shoot them for food for our family, but I didn't eat them myself.

Since then I've tried rabbit meat again, and I find it's just as good as I remember it, but at least for that day the pleasure of eating rabbit was gone for me.

In looking back, I suppose that was the day I grew up. That day I saw the dividing line between what had gone before and what lay ahead, between what I had experienced and what I could envision. Since then I've witnessed other things that weren't pleasant, things that would give kids nightmares, but none had the lasting impact on me that that day did. Death looked me in the face that day in May, 1936, and I was horrified, not so much afraid of it happening to me as I was afraid of becoming instrumental in causing it to happen to somebody else. Maturity, I think, is the growing awareness or responsibility especially to ourselves but to others, too. We aren't always comfortable with having to be responsible for ourselves and our lives, but much more oppressive is the assumption of responsibility for others. That's why fathering children is so important; it's an obligation that can't be wished or given away. One assumes it and hopes that what he does for his children will help them to escape some of what we went through. And as for me I hope that what I do won't be judged too harshly by whoever does the judging.

We're told that men can judge deeds only; it's up to God to judge intentions. I suppose the intentions that day were honorable for the most part: to protect crops and, by extension, family. But at twelve years of age, all I could see was the deed: that horribly extended period of killing and bloodshed that in just a few years was repeated and amplified in World War II in the lives of men. But, finally, I'm afraid that the deeds we judge others by are also the ones we are judged by. Is this what it means to stand naked before one's creator, with nothing mitigating the punishment?

Afterward

"Dust in the Wind" is not autobiography. I was born too late to experience the "dirty thirties." However, I spent the summers of 1952 and 1954, and from October, 1956 through August, 1957 on a farm northwest of La Crosse, Kansas where I heard many stories of the blowing dust and assimilated many of them into my consciousness.

I never went on a rabbit drive. During the winter of 1959-1960 I was working in the service station of the Farmer's Co-op in La Crosse when I heard about a rabbit drive on a Sunday. I worked every Sunday from 8:00 a.m. until 9:00 p.m., so I couldn't go. But I heard about it, and I have tried to capture what it was like or what I was told it was like. I think I'm glad I was working.

Ben, eighteen years older than I, would be 77 now. He and his generation lived through an economic time that offered no shoring for their lives; all was quicksand. Men went without work for years, and many left home to ride the rails in search of jobs. Those who had farms to live on were luckier but not by much. The accompanying photographs, taken during the 1930s, show the influence of the dust bowl conditions on people's lives. Today, farmers are more intelligent about the needs of the land, and they don't farm the same way. In addition, government programs instituted during the 30s, 40s, and 50s offered some relief. There are many more trees today in Kansas than there were during the 30s, thanks to government programs. I hope the dust bowl conditions never return.

About the Author

Don Richardson is a member of the English Department at Phoenix College in Arizona where he teaches English Composition, British Literature, and Introduction to Shakespeare. For more than a decade he also taught Children's Literature which led him to explore many fine writers and works. His favorite books are those written for young adult readers as they challenge readers to discover positive solutions for their life challenges. Although he has written several manuscripts, this is his first to be published. His hobbies are singing, reading, cooking, gardening, and woodworking. He also does volunteer work in the community.